The Tale of
Squirrel Nutkin

The Tale of
Squirrel Nutkin

by Beatrix Potter

DERRYDALE BOOKS
New York

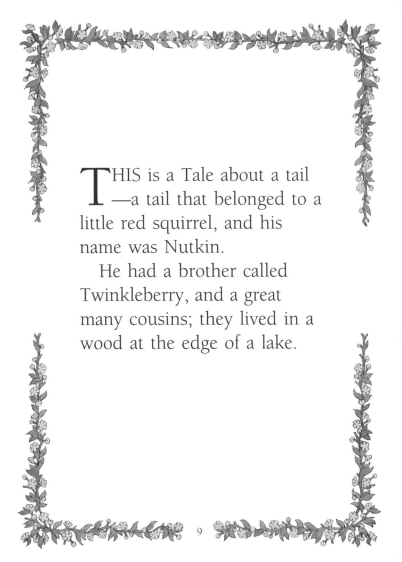

THIS is a Tale about a tail —a tail that belonged to a little red squirrel, and his name was Nutkin.

He had a brother called Twinkleberry, and a great many cousins; they lived in a wood at the edge of a lake.

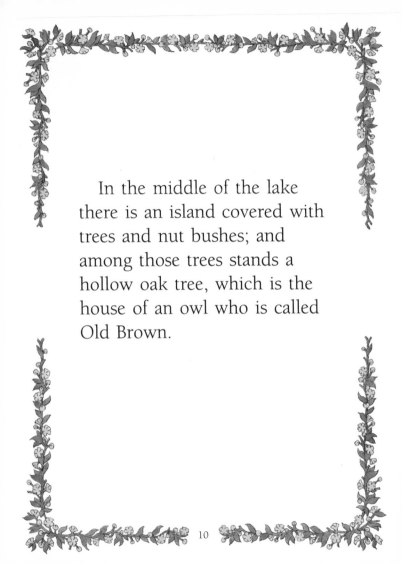

In the middle of the lake there is an island covered with trees and nut bushes; and among those trees stands a hollow oak tree, which is the house of an owl who is called Old Brown.

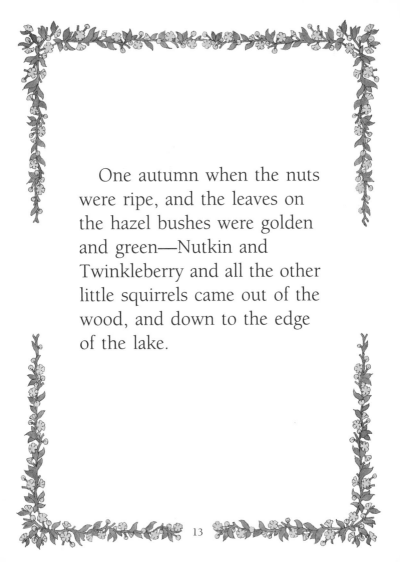

One autumn when the nuts were ripe, and the leaves on the hazel bushes were golden and green—Nutkin and Twinkleberry and all the other little squirrels came out of the wood, and down to the edge of the lake.

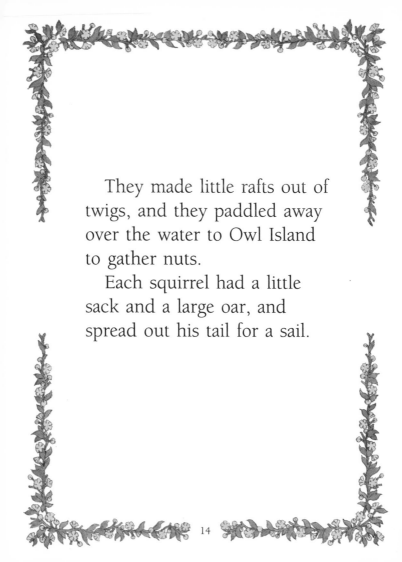

They made little rafts out of twigs, and they paddled away over the water to Owl Island to gather nuts.

Each squirrel had a little sack and a large oar, and spread out his tail for a sail.

They also took with them
an offering of three fat mice as
a present for Old Brown, and
put them down upon his
doorstep.

Then Twinkleberry and the
other little squirrels each made
a low bow, and said politely:

"Old Mr. Brown, will you
favor us with permission to
gather nuts on your island?"

But Nutkin was excessively
impertinent in his manners.
He bobbed up and down like
a little red *cherry,* singing—

Riddle me, riddle me, rot-tot-tote!
A little wee man, in a red, red coat!
A staff in his hand, and a stone in his
    throat;
If you'll tell me this riddle, I'll give you
    a groat.

Now this riddle is as old as
the hills; Mr. Brown paid no
attention whatever to Nutkin.

He shut his eyes obstinately
and went to sleep.

The squirrels filled their
little sacks with nuts, and
sailed away home in the
evening.

But next morning they all came back again to Owl Island; and Twinkleberry and the others brought a fine fat mole, and laid it on the stone in front of Old Brown's doorway, and said—

"Mr. Brown, will you favor us with your gracious permission to gather some more nuts?"

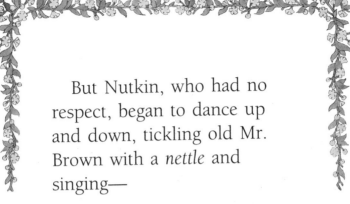

But Nutkin, who had no
respect, began to dance up
and down, tickling old Mr.
Brown with a *nettle* and
singing—

> Old Mr. B! Riddle-me-ree!
> Hitty Pitty within the wall,
> Hitty Pitty without the wall;
> If you touch Hitty Pitty,
> Hitty Pitty will bite you!

Mr. Brown woke up
suddenly and carried the mole
into his house.

He shut the door in Nutkin's face. Presently a little thread of blue *smoke* from a wood fire came up from the top of the tree, and Nutkin peeped through the keyhole and sang—

A house full, a hole full!
And you cannot gather a bowl-full!

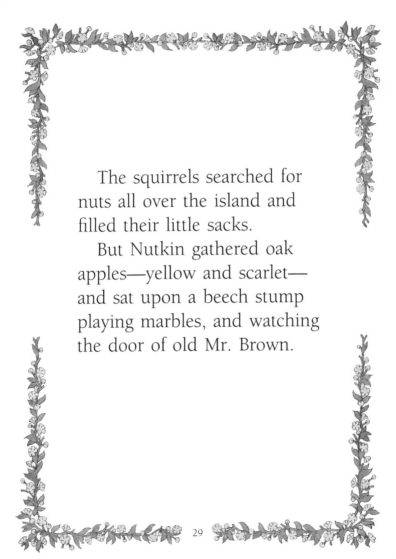

The squirrels searched for nuts all over the island and filled their little sacks.

But Nutkin gathered oak apples—yellow and scarlet—and sat upon a beech stump playing marbles, and watching the door of old Mr. Brown.

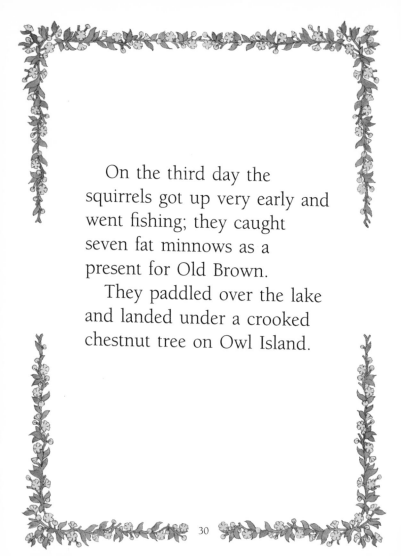

On the third day the squirrels got up very early and went fishing; they caught seven fat minnows as a present for Old Brown.

They paddled over the lake and landed under a crooked chestnut tree on Owl Island.

Twinkleberry and six other little squirrels each carried a fat minnow; but Nutkin, who had no nice manners, brought no present at all. He ran in front, singing—

The man in the wilderness said to me,
"How many strawberries grow in the
    sea?"
I answered him as I thought good—
"As many red herrings as grow in the
    wood."

But old Mr. Brown took no interest in riddles—not even when the answer was provided for him.

On the fourth day the squirrels brought a present of six fat beetles, which were as good as plums in *plum pudding* for Old Brown. Each beetle was wrapped up carefully in a dock leaf, fastened with a pine needle pin.

But Nutkin sang as rudely as ever—

Old Mr. B! Riddle-me-ree!
Flour of England, fruit of Spain,
Met together in a shower of rain;
Put in a bag tied round with a string,
If you'll tell me this riddle, I'll give you
a ring!

Which was ridiculous of Nutkin, because he had not got any ring to give to Old Brown.

The other squirrels hunted
up and down the nut bushes;
but Nutkin gathered robin's
pincushions off a brier bush,
and stuck them full of pine
needle pins.

On the fifth day the squirrels brought a present of wild honey; it was so sweet and sticky that they licked their fingers as they put it down upon the stone. They had stolen it out of a bumble *bees'* nest on the tippity top of the hill.

But Nutkin skipped up and down, singing—

Hum-a-bum! Buzz! Buzz! Hum-a-bum buzz!
    As I went over Tipple-tine
    I met a flock of bonny swine;
Some yellow-nacked, some yellow backed!
    They were the very bonniest swine
    That e'er went over Tipple-tine.

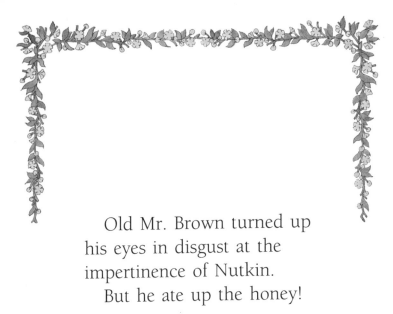

Old Mr. Brown turned up
his eyes in disgust at the
impertinence of Nutkin.

But he ate up the honey!

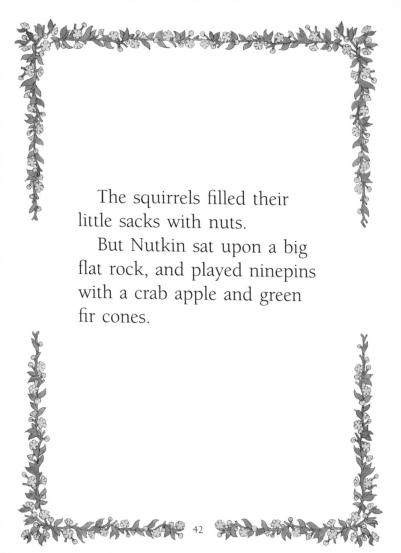

The squirrels filled their
little sacks with nuts.

But Nutkin sat upon a big
flat rock, and played ninepins
with a crab apple and green
fir cones.

On the sixth day, which was Saturday, the squirrels came again for the last time; they brought a new-laid *egg* in a little rush basket as a last parting present for Old Brown.

But Nutkin ran in front laughing, and shouting—

Humpty Dumpty lies in the beck,
With a white counterpane round his
    neck,
Forty doctors and forty wrights,
Cannot put Humpty Dumpty to rights!

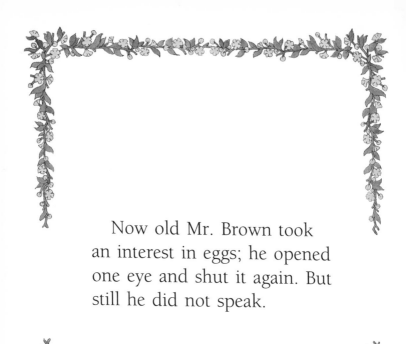

Now old Mr. Brown took
an interest in eggs; he opened
one eye and shut it again. But
still he did not speak.

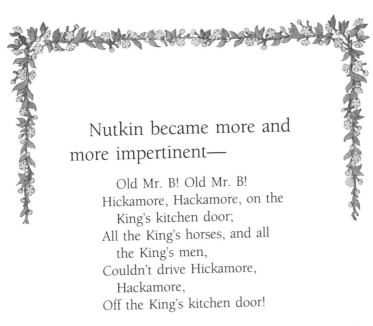

Nutkin became more and more impertinent—

Old Mr. B! Old Mr. B!
Hickamore, Hackamore, on the
    King's kitchen door;
All the King's horses, and all
    the King's men,
Couldn't drive Hickamore,
    Hackamore,
Off the King's kitchen door!

Nutkin danced up and down like a *sunbeam;* but still Old Brown said nothing at all.

Nutkin began again—

Arthur O'Bower has broken his band,
He comes roaring up the land!
The King of Scots with all his power,
Cannot turn Arthur of the Bower!

Nutkin made a whirring noise to sound like the *wind*, and he took a running jump right onto the head of Old Brown! . . .

Then all at once there was a flutterment and a scufflement and a loud "Squeak!"

The other squirrels scuttered away into the bushes.

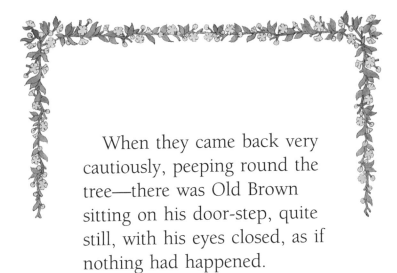

When they came back very cautiously, peeping round the tree—there was Old Brown sitting on his door-step, quite still, with his eyes closed, as if nothing had happened.

* * * * * * * *

But Nutkin was in his waist-coat pocket!

This looks like the end of
the story; but it isn't.

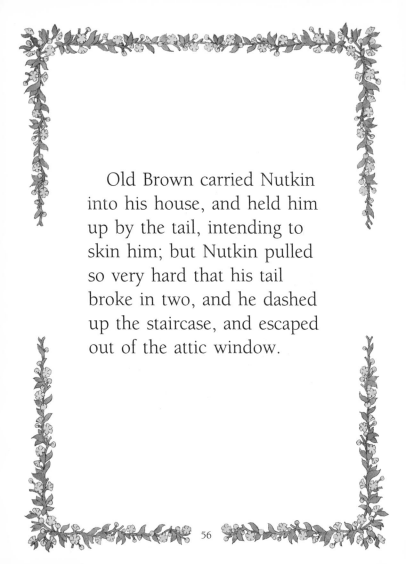

Old Brown carried Nutkin into his house, and held him up by the tail, intending to skin him; but Nutkin pulled so very hard that his tail broke in two, and he dashed up the staircase, and escaped out of the attic window.

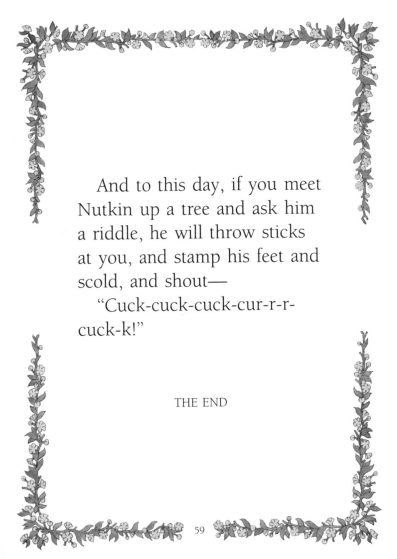

And to this day, if you meet Nutkin up a tree and ask him a riddle, he will throw sticks at you, and stamp his feet and scold, and shout—

"Cuck-cuck-cuck-cur-r-r-cuck-k!"

THE END

ABOUT BEATRIX POTTER

Born in London in 1866, Beatrix Potter spent a lonely childhood. Her well-to-do parents did not send her to school, but instead had her taught by governesses at home. Her only friend was her younger brother Bertram. On vacations in Scotland, she and Bertram escaped into a world of farms, woods, and fields, where they delighted in watching and collecting plants, animals, and insects.

In London, yearning for the country, and the fascinating little animals she loved, Beatrix kept small pets in her nursery—a rabbit, some mice, snails, and even a hedgehog—and began to draw them, as well as plants and flowers she had seen in the countryside.

Out of these drawings grew her illustrated stories about rabbits and other small animals. They began as letters to children, then became published books. The stories were so popular that at the age of thirty-six, Beatrix Potter found herself a successful children's author. She continued to write and illustrate her delightful tales, eventually more than two dozen, and successive generations of children have cherished them.

Editorial Note

The language of Beatrix Potter's stories includes certain British words or phrases which may be unfamiliar to today's American children. Therefore, in a few cases, the text has been altered slightly to make it more comprehensible. The changes, however, have been kept to a minimum to retain the charm of the original.

Dedication

A STORY FOR NORAH

"About Beatrix Potter"
Copyright © 1992 by Outlet Book Company, Inc.
All rights reserved.

This 1992 edition is published by Derrydale Books, distributed by
Outlet Book Company, Inc., a Random House Company,
225 Park Avenue South, New York, New York 10003.

Printed and bound in the United States of America

Library of Congress Cataloging-in-Publication Data

Potter, Beatrix, 1866–1943.
    The tale of Squirrel Nutkin / by Beatrix Potter.
       p.   cm.
    Summary: Squirrel Nutkin would rather ask an old owl riddles than
gather nuts with the other squirrels.
    ISBN 0–517–07239–4
    [1. Squirrels—Fiction.]   I. Title.
PZ7.P85Tas   1992
[E]—dc20
                                              91–32189
                                                     CIP
                                                       AC

For this edition of The Tale of Squirrel Nutkin:
Cover and interior design: Clair Moritz
Production supervision: Helen Marra and Ellen Reed
Editorial supervision: Claire Booss

8   7   6   5   4   3   2   1